For my friend, Arline, and her successful career
of teaching and inspiring inner-city kids.

For my husband, Steve, and our lovable
dog, Sophie, who patiently waits to play ball
whenever I sit down to draw.

For all the kids who have dreams of making their
environment a better place, and who make that
dream happen—like Rosa and Miguel.

MASCOT KIDS!

www.mascotbooks.com

The Pear Tree

For more information, please contact:
Mascot Books
620 Herndon Parkway, Suite 320
Herndon, VA 20170
info@mascotbooks.com

Library of Congress Control Number: 2021904950

CPSIA Code: PRT0621A
ISBN-13: 978-1-64543-870-0

Printed in the United States

The Pear Tree

Beth Dupree and Arline McKeen

Illustrated by Beth Dupree

My name is Rosa. I live with my mother and brother, Miguel, in a big city with lots of tall buildings. We live on the second floor of our building, and our neighbors, Mr. Tony, Mrs. Carmen, Maribel, and José, live on the first floor.

Our neighborhood is nice, but my mother, Miguel, and I would love to have a nice yard with grass, flowers, and trees. My mother could even have a garden for fresh vegetables.

One night, Mama got me thinking!

We had just finished our supper and were eating pears for dessert. The pears reminded us of our visits with our grandmother, and the beautiful pear tree she kept in her backyard. Mama said, "We got delicious fresh pears from the trees."

After we finished our dessert, I had an idea! Miguel and I would save the seeds from our pears so we could take them outside and plant them.

I ran to the front window and looked down. *Oh no!* I thought. There was no room to plant seeds.

Next, I ran to the back balcony and looked for a place for our pear seeds. We couldn't plant them there either. There was nothing but sidewalks on either side of our building.

As I helped Mama with the supper dishes, I started daydreaming about planting seeds to grow a pear tree.

I couldn't sleep. The noise from the fire
engine sirens and the people talking in
the street was keeping me awake.

I wanted a pear tree, but where could we
plant one in our neighborhood?

Finally, I fell asleep and dreamed
about beautiful pear trees.

The next morning, I had an idea. Miguel and I could look for a place to plant the seeds on our way to school. I carefully put the seeds into my backpack, along with a popsicle stick and a spoon for digging.

Miguel and I usually talk and play on our way to school, but today we were busy looking for a place to plant our seeds. We walked around a corner, and suddenly Miguel shouted, "Look!"

He had found a big, vacant lot. There was a lot of junk, but after some searching, we found a spot for our pear trees. We dug a hole and planted our seeds, then stuck the popsicle stick beside it.

Each day after school we watered our pear seeds, waiting for something to happen. A few days later, we were so excited to see a skinny little sprout growing from the seeds!

One day, after Miguel and I watered the sprout, our neighbors, Mrs. Rodriguez and Mrs. Watson, walked into the vacant lot. They wanted to know what we were doing.

I showed them our little garden, and told them, "We planted pear seeds because we wanted to grow a pear tree like our grandmother."

"What a wonderful idea! We need more trees in our neighborhood, and fruit trees most of all," said Mrs. Watson.

As we left the lot, Mrs. Watson said to Mrs. Rodriguez, "If our neighbors pitched in and helped clean this lot, we could plant even more trees."

"Yes," replied Mrs. Rodriguez, "then we'd have a nice shady park for all of the neighborhood to enjoy."

Later that summer after returning from a long visit with our grandmother, Miguel and I went to check on our pear tree. We couldn't wait to see how much it had grown.

As I rounded the corner, I couldn't believe my eyes! The old vacant lot was now a beautiful park.

Children were running and playing everywhere. There were swings, seesaws, and balloons. And, best of all, right in the middle of the park was our pear tree, with ripe fruit hanging from the branches.

As we ran into the park, Miguel and I saw a sign in front of our pear tree that said, "This park is dedicated to Rosa and Miguel." It was all because we wanted a pear tree like our grandmother.

About Beth Dupree

I am a retired art educator who taught all levels, from kindergarten to college, throughout my career. During my professional teaching career, and since my retirement, I have also been fortunate to exhibit my own works of fabric and acrylic collage on canvas. I still work in my studio, painting and working on illustrations, watching my pictures help stories come to life.

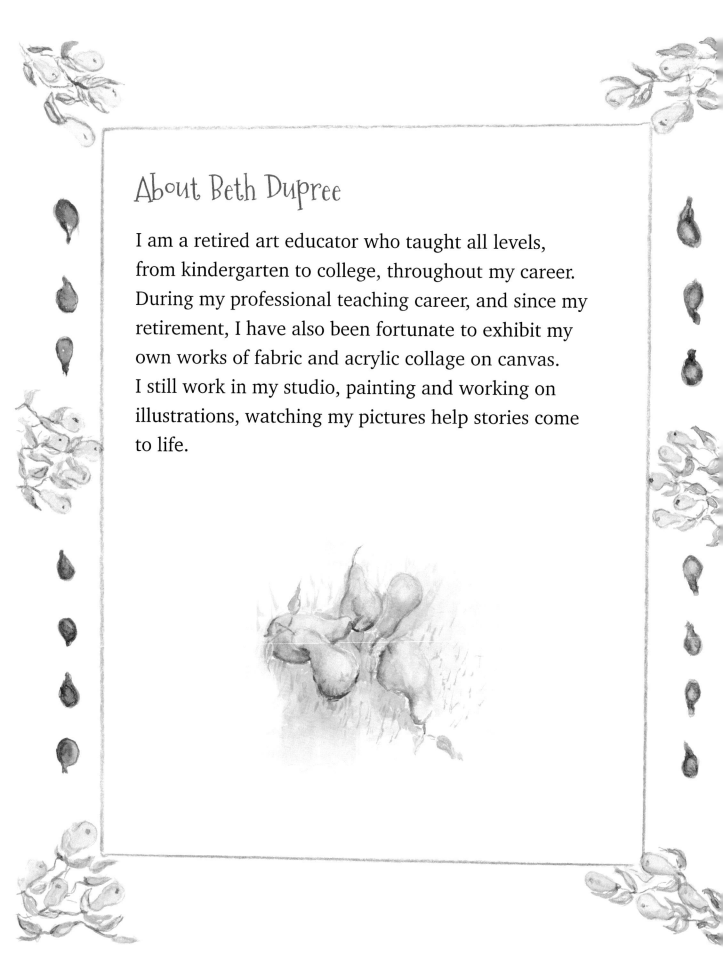

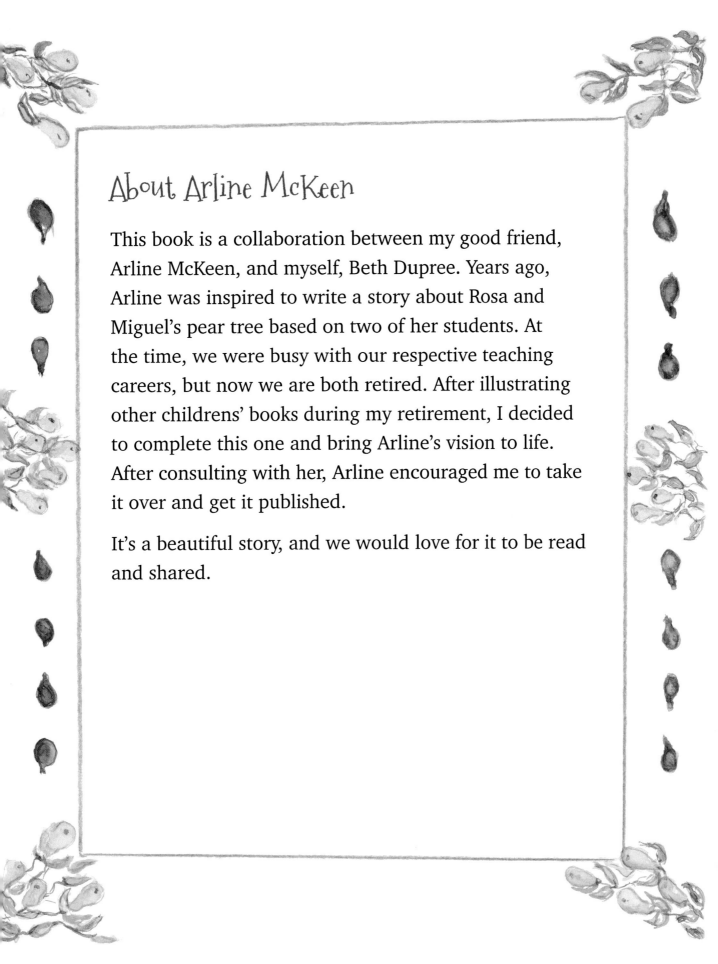

About Arline McKeen

This book is a collaboration between my good friend, Arline McKeen, and myself, Beth Dupree. Years ago, Arline was inspired to write a story about Rosa and Miguel's pear tree based on two of her students. At the time, we were busy with our respective teaching careers, but now we are both retired. After illustrating other childrens' books during my retirement, I decided to complete this one and bring Arline's vision to life. After consulting with her, Arline encouraged me to take it over and get it published.

It's a beautiful story, and we would love for it to be read and shared.